Let's Have a DOG PARTY!

by Mikela Prevost

VIKING

This is Frank's spot.

It's his favorite spot
in Kate's house.
More than his bed,
more than his bowl.
Frank's spot is warm
and soft and perfect
for napping.

But not today.

Happy Birthday, Frank!

"We need to get you ready!"
yelled Kate.

Frank was not ready for this.

Frank watched his bed disappear.

And then his bowl.

Frank really wanted
his spot now.

It had to be under
these things.

"Hey!
Frank wants to
open his presents!"

"Look, Frank!
It's your ball!"

"Look, Frank!
It's your
squeaky toy!"

"Look, Frank!
It's a dried-up lizard
we found outside!"

"Wait!"
Kate yelled.

"We have to sing 'Happy Birthday'!"

Kate and her friends sang . . . **LOUD**.

Frank's ears hurt.

They danced in circles.
Frank felt dizzy.

He had to get out of there!

"Look!

Frank wants to play hide-and-seek!"

Frank found a new spot.
It was cold and dark
and smelled like feet.
Not perfect for napping.
But at least it was quiet.

Found You!

Kate gasped.

Frank could hear
kids whispering
and then walking
out the front door.

Then he heard Kate's footsteps.

Kate patted the ground.

"Frank, will you come out, please?"

Frank crawled out slowly.

"I'm sorry, boy," Kate said.
Frank gave her a kiss.

"I have one last surprise.

Can you smell it?"

"Happy Birthday, Frank!"

Now this was a party Frank liked.

This book is for my favorite party people—Lily, Abby, Jude, and Cameron.
And also Lashawn—who always stays to help clean up. — MP

VIKING
Penguin Young Readers Group
An imprint of Penguin Random House LLC
375 Hudson Street
New York, New York 10014

First published in the United States of America by Viking,
an imprint of Penguin Random House LLC, 2019

LIBRARY OF CONGRESS CATALOGING-IN-PUBLICATION DATA IS AVAILABLE
ISBN: 9780451481177

Printed in China

1 3 5 7 9 10 8 6 4 2

Set in Pluto   Book Design by Mariam Quraishi

The art for this book was rendered in watercolor,
acryla gouache, and colored pencils with a bit of collage.